Published in 2022 by Enslow Publishing, LLC
29 East 21st Street
New York, NY 10010

Copyright © 2022 Enslow Publishing, LLC
All rights reserved.

Produced for Rosen by Ruth Owen Books
Designer: Emma Randall
Photos courtesy of Ruth Owen Books and Shutterstock

Cataloging-in-Publication Data

Names: Owen, Ruth.
Title: Let's celebrate with more Valentine's Day origami / Ruth Owen.
Description: New York : Enslow Publishing, 2022. | Series: Let's celebrate with origami | Includes glossary and index.
Identifiers: ISBN 9781978526754 (pbk.) | ISBN 9781978526778 (library bound) | ISBN 9781978526761 (6 pack) | ISBN 9781978526785 (ebook)
Subjects: LCSH: Origami--Juvenile literature. | Valentine decorations--Juvenile literature.
Classification: LCC TT870.O946 2022 | DDC 736'.982--dc23

All rights reserved. No part of this book may be reproduced in any form without permission in writing from the publisher, except by a reviewer.

Manufactured in the United States of America

CPSIA compliance information: Batch #CWENS22: For further information contact Enslow Publishing, New York, New York at 1-800-398-2504

Find us on

Contents

Folding with Love 4

Origami Tips 6

A Striped Love Heart 8

Paper Roses 10

Make a Winged Heart...................................... 14

Tell a Fortune 18

Origami Envelope 22

A Valentine Teddy Bear 26

Glossary, Index, Websites 32

Folding with Love

When Valentine's Day comes around, show the people you love how much you care by folding them a **unique** and fun **origami** gift.

Origami is a popular art form and hobby. In fact, people have been doing origami around the world for centuries. The word "origami" comes from Japan. It means "folding paper" in Japanese.

If you like origami, you will love the selection of models in this book that can be created as gifts for Valentine's Day. All you need to do is make careful folds and you will be able to create hearts, an envelope for a card or love letter, and even a cute paper teddy bear. You will also be able to tell a friend's **fortune**!

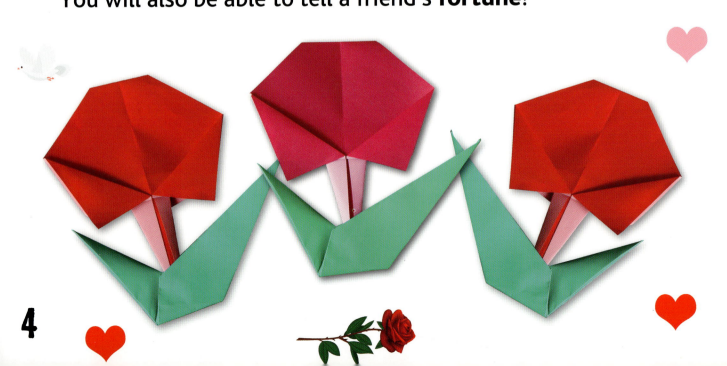

4

Origami Tips

Here are some tips to get you started on your origami model making.

Tip 1
Read all the instructions carefully and look at the pictures. Make sure you understand what's required before you begin a fold. Don't rush; be patient. Work slowly and carefully.

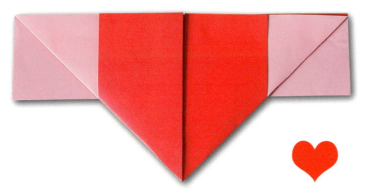

Tip 2
Folding a piece of paper sounds easy, but it can be tricky to get neat, accurate folds. The more you practice, the easier it becomes.

Tip 3
If an instruction says "crease," make the crease as flat as possible. The flatter the creases, the better the model. You can make a sharp crease by running a plastic ruler along the edge of the paper.

Tip 4
Sometimes, at first, your models may look a little crumpled. Don't give up! The more models you make, the better you will get at folding and creasing.

When it comes to origami, practice makes perfect!

The beautiful paper origami heart and rose on this page were made by an experienced model maker. They were created by making lots of tricky folds. This book will show you how to make your own paper hearts and roses. Keep practicing your origami and you'll soon be making complicated models like the ones shown here.

You can use the origami hearts you make to create Valentine's cards. Try making the hearts in different sizes. For example, from a small piece of paper that's 3 inches (7.5 cm) square, you can make two tiny candy-striped hearts that are each just 2 inches (5 cm) wide. That's perfect for decorating a card!

A Striped Love Heart

No matter what language you speak, when you see a heart, you know it means love! In fact, this simple shape is the **symbol** for love all over the world. Sometimes a heart is even used in writing to take the place of the word "love."

Try making these cute candy-striped love hearts, and this Valentine's Day, show the people you love how you feel with some wonderful origami.

To make striped love hearts, you will need:

Squares of paper that are white on one side and red, pink, or purple on the other side

Scissors

(Origami paper is sometimes colored on both sides or white on one side.)

STEP 1:
Cut a square of paper in half. Take one half and place it colored side down. Fold the paper in half, crease, and then unfold.

STEP 2:
Now fold the bottom of the paper in half so it meets the center crease, and crease well. Then do the same with the top half of the paper.

STEP 3:
Unfold the bottom half of the model. Then fold up the bottom again to meet the bottom crease you've just made in step 2.

STEP 4:
Turn the model over. Now fold it in half from left to right, crease, and unfold.

Next, fold up the right-hand side of the model so it lines up with the center crease you've just made, and crease hard. Then repeat on the left-hand side.

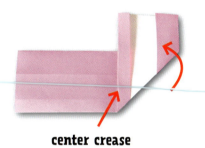

center crease

STEP 5:
Turn the model over and it should look like this.

Now fold down the four top corners of the model, and crease hard.

Flip the model over and your striped love heart is ready to go! You can make hearts in many different sizes.

This heart was made with paper that's red on one side and pink on the other.

9

Paper Roses

In ancient Greece, a red rose was the symbol for the goddess of love, Aphrodite. It was also the symbol for Venus, who was the Roman goddess of love. Today, red roses are still a symbol for love—whether that's a dozen arranged in a big bouquet or a beautiful single red rose.

This Valentine's Day, try making a long-lasting red rose that won't die after just a few days. Follow these instructions to create a **romantic** single red rose. Or you can make a whole bunch of paper roses in rainbow colors!

To make a rose, you will need:

- One sheet of paper that's red or pink (the paper can be white on one side or a lighter shade of red or pink)
- One sheet of green paper
- Glue

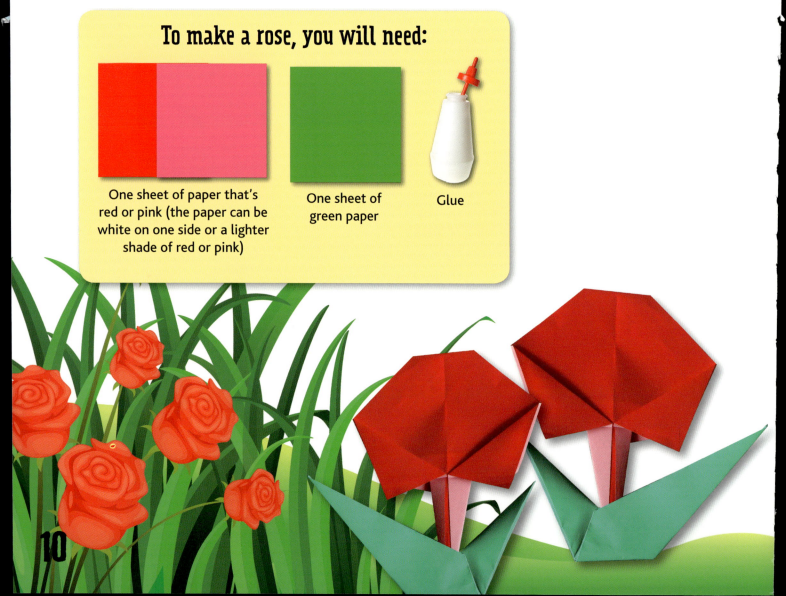

STEP 1:
Place the paper with the color you want for your rose facing up. Fold the paper in half, crease, and unfold.

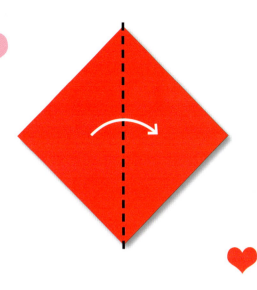

STEP 2:
Now fold in the two sides of the paper so that they meet at the center crease to make a kite shape. Crease well.

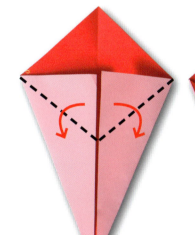

STEP 3:
Fold down the two flaps along the dotted lines, and crease well.

STEP 4:
Turn the model over. Fold up the bottom point to meet the top point, and crease hard. Then fold the bottom point back down again, creating a small pleat, and crease hard.

11

STEP 5:
Fold down the two points created by the pleat along the dotted lines, and crease hard.

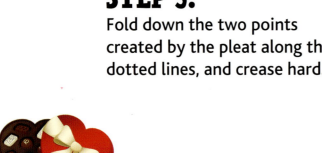

Next, fold in the right-hand side of the rose's stem so the edge lines up with the crease in the center of the stem. As you make this fold, open out the folded-down point at the top of the stem and flatten it to create a triangle. Then repeat on the left-hand side.

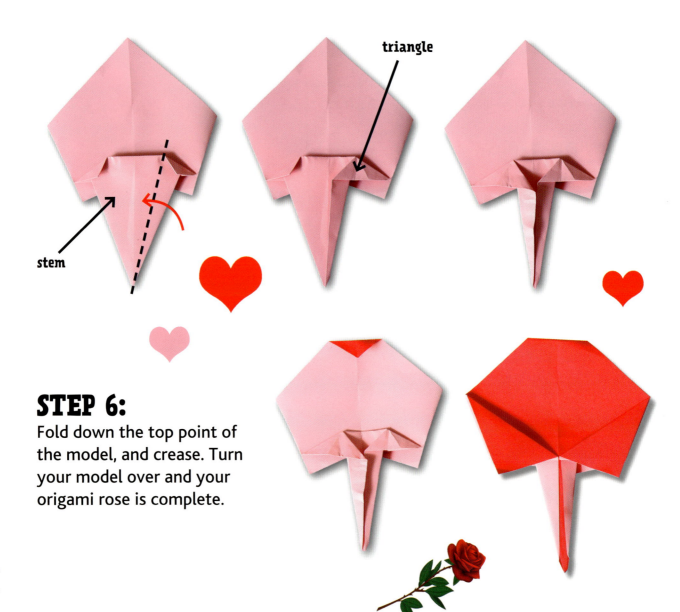

STEP 6:
Fold down the top point of the model, and crease. Turn your model over and your origami rose is complete.

STEP 7:
To make leaves for the rose, place the green paper colored side down. Repeat steps 1 and 2 to make a kite shape.

STEP 8:
Fold in the two right-hand edges along the dotted lines so that they meet at the center crease, and crease well.

STEP 9:
Fold the model in half by folding down the top of the model along the center crease, and crease well. Then fold up the right-hand side of the model along the dotted line, and crease hard.

STEP 10:
Finally, slide the stem of the rose into the center of the leaves and add a little glue to hold the rose in place.

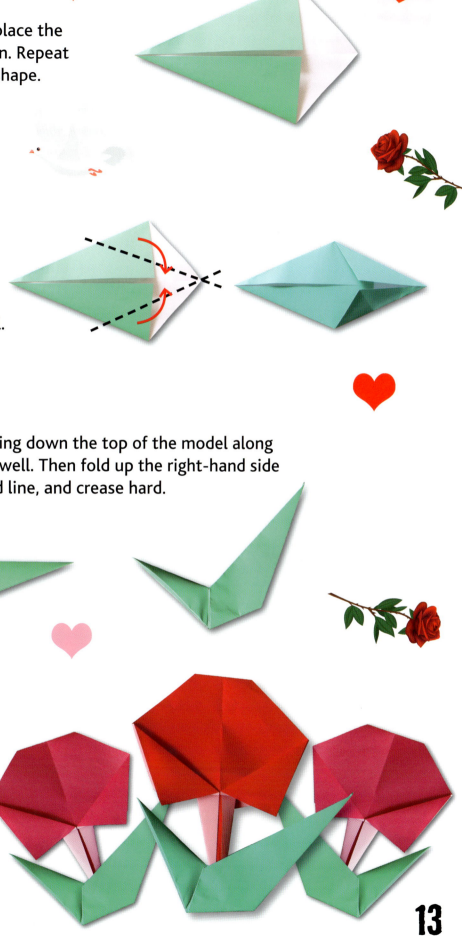

13

Make a Winged Heart

Why are hearts sometimes shown with birdlike wings? No one can say for sure, but maybe it symbolizes a heart flying, because it is filled with the happiness of falling in love!

If you enjoyed making the striped love heart, you will have fun making these winged hearts.

They are a wonderful decoration for a Valentine's Day card and are very simple to make. You can use paper that's white on one side to have white wings, or choose paper that is a different color on each side to make a multicolored winged heart.

To make a winged heart, you will need:

One sheet of paper that's red or pink (the paper can be white on one side or a lighter shade of red or pink)

STEP 1:
Choose the color of your heart. Then place the paper with this color facing down. Fold the paper in half, crease, and unfold. Then fold the paper in half in the other direction, crease, and unfold.

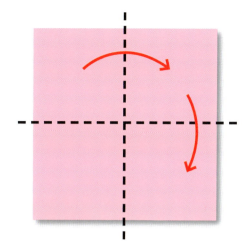

STEP 2:
Fold up the bottom half of the paper to meet the center crease, and crease well.

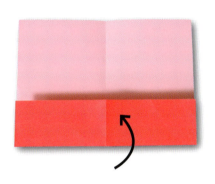

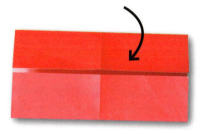

Then repeat on the top half of the model.

STEP 3:
Turn the model over. Then fold up the right-hand side of the model, and crease well.

Repeat on the left-hand side of the model. Your model should now look like this.

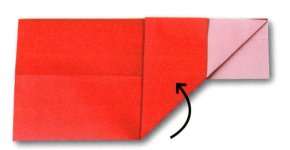

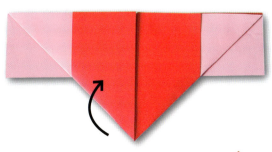

15

STEP 4:

Turn the model back over. Now fold down the top section along the dotted line, and crease hard.

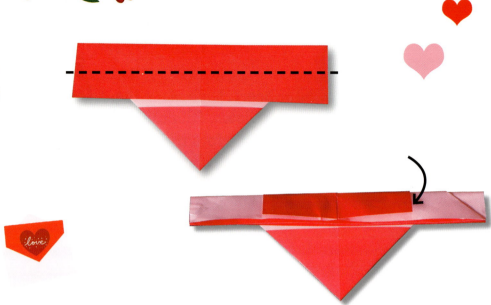

STEP 5:

Now take hold of the small flap on the right-hand side of the model, and gently open up the flap so it lies flat on your work surface. As you do this, you will see a small triangle forming. Gently flatten that triangle against the model.

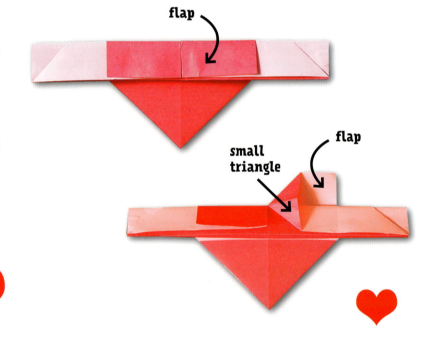

Then repeat on the other side of the model.

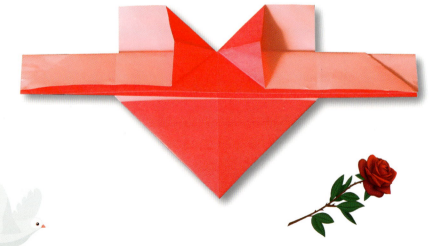

STEP 6:

Fold over the model's two top points. Then fold in the two points at the sides of the model.

STEP 7:

Turn the model over, and your origami winged heart is complete!

17

Tell a Fortune

Did you know it's possible to tell your fortune with origami? People have been making this fun fortune-teller model for many years. So follow the instructions and then try playing the game on page 21.

Will the fortune-teller reveal who your friends will marry? Perhaps it might warn a friend that his or her Valentine should be avoided!

You can think up your own fortunes to write inside your model, and then test them out on your friends.
Make sure you take a turn, too!

To make a fortune-teller, you will need:

One sheet of paper in your choice of color

A black marker

18

STEP 1:

Place the paper colored side down. Fold in half from side to side, crease, and unfold. Then fold in half from top to bottom, crease, and unfold.

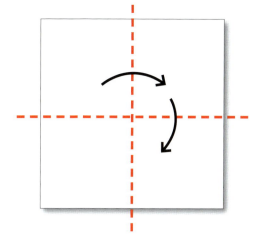

Now fold the paper in half diagonally from side to side, crease, and unfold. Repeat from top to bottom.

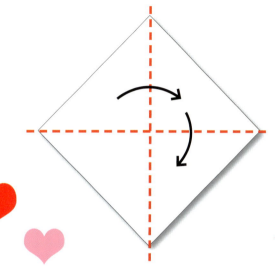

STEP 2:

Fold the four points of the paper into the center, creasing each edge well.

STEP 3:

Turn the model over. Now write your fortunes on the model. Write one fortune in each of the eight sections.

19

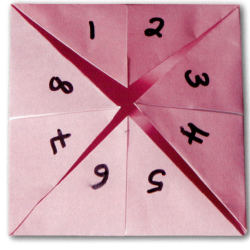

STEP 4:

Now fold each of the four points of the model into the center, creasing each edge well.

Then write a number from 1 to 8 on each of the eight sections.

STEP 5:

Turn the model over. Now write a color on each of the four sections, or flaps.

Then gently open out the four flaps.

STEP 6:

When you turn the model over, it should now look like this. Your fortune-teller is ready to go!

20

Tell a Valentine Fortune

Follow these instructions to have fun with your fortune-teller on Valentine's Day.

1. Slide your thumbs and forefingers into the back of the fortune-teller, so that you can open and close the four sections.

2. With the fortune-teller closed, ask your friend to name their valentine. Now you will tell the couple's fortune.

3. Ask your friend to choose one of the colors on the fortune-teller. For example, BLUE. Now move your fingers in and out, opening and closing the fortune-teller once for each letter...B...L...U...E.

4. Ask your friend to look into the fortune-teller and choose a number, for example, 4. Then open and close the fortune-teller four times.

5. Now ask your friend to look into the fortune-teller again and choose another number, for example, 8.

6. Finally, open up the fortune-teller and look under flap number 8. The fortune for your friend and their valentine is KISS!

Origami Envelope

Do you want to send a special message to someone this Valentine's Day? Then make this origami envelope and put your Valentine's card or love letter inside.

You can make the envelope from any type of paper. Try using gift-wrapping paper to create a truly unique design. You can make your envelope from a square or rectangular piece of paper. Just follow the instructions, and either shape will work. You can also make your envelope in any size. For example, a piece of printer paper will make an envelope that measures approximately 5 inches by 4 inches (13 cm x 10 cm).

To make origami envelopes, you will need:

Paper in your choice of colors

STEP 1:

Place the paper colored side down, and fold up the bottom half of the paper. Crease well.

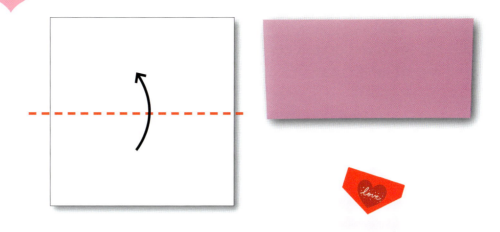

STEP 2:

Fold down the top layer of paper along the dotted line, and crease.

Now fold the top layer of paper back up again along the dotted line, crease, and unfold.

STEP 3:

Now fold up the top layer of paper again, so the edge meets the last crease you made in step 2, and crease.

Then fold up the top layer of paper a second time along the dotted line, and crease.

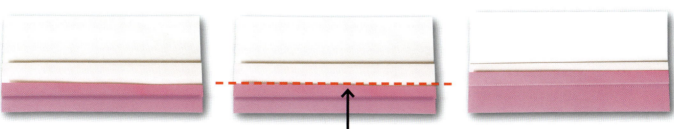

Fold up this section again.

23

STEP 4:

Fold in the two bottom corners of the model, and crease hard.

STEP 5:

Now fold in the two sides of the model along the dotted lines, and crease hard.

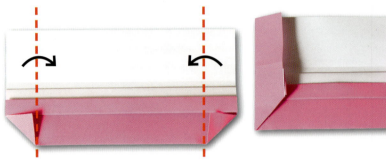

STEP 6:

Next, unfold the two sides of the model and fold down the bottom corners. Fold up the center flap of the model too.

Now take hold of the top right-hand layer of paper and open it out. As you do this, a triangle will form at the bottom of the model. Gently squash the triangle flat.

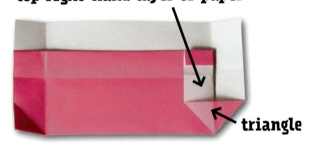

Then repeat on the left-hand side. Your model should now look like this.

STEP 7:

Fold the center flap of the model back down again, and crease.

24

STEP 8:
Fold in the right-hand side of the model. As you do this, allow the triangle at the bottom to unfold and flatten. Now tuck the triangle-shaped section marked by the dotted lines inside the model to secure the right-hand side of the envelope. Repeat on the left-hand side.

Tuck this triangle inside the model.

triangles tucked inside model

STEP 9:
Fold down the top of the model along the dotted line so that edge A meets edge B, crease, and then unfold.

Now fold down the model's two top corners so they meet the crease you've just made, and crease well.

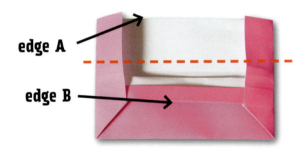

edge A

edge B

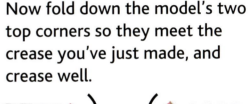

STEP 10:
Next, unfold the top right-hand corner. Then, using the creases you've made previously, slide and tuck the right-hand side of the model inside the envelope. Repeat on the other side.

STEP 11:
Your origami envelope is now ready to use.

To close the envelope, tuck the top edge of the envelope inside the center bar-shaped section.

The top right-hand side of the image has slid inside the envelope.

bar-shaped section

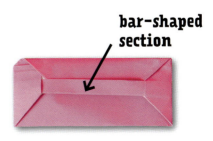

25

A Valentine Teddy Bear

In this final project, you can learn how to make a cute origami teddy bear that's holding a heart. You can even write your own Valentine's Day message on the heart.

Your valentine will be thrilled to receive this special handmade paper greeting. Happy Valentine's Day!

To make a teddy and love heart, you will need:

- One sheet of paper that's orange, brown, or yellow
- One sheet of paper that's pink or red
- A black marker
- Scissors
- Glue

STEP 1:

We've used orange paper that has spots on its reverse. Begin by placing the paper colored side down. Fold in half from one side to the other, crease, and unfold. Then fold in half from top to bottom, crease, and unfold.

Next, fold in the two side points so they meet in the center, and crease.

STEP 2:

Then fold in the two sides of the model again, and crease well.

STEP 3:

Unfold all the creases you've made and lay the paper flat. Now fold the left-hand side of the model over so that the point meets the middle crease on the right-hand side, and crease.

Now, fold the left-hand point back again, and crease.

Make the same folds on the right-hand side of the model, so your model looks like this.

27

STEP 4:
Now fold in the side points of the model along the dotted lines, and crease.

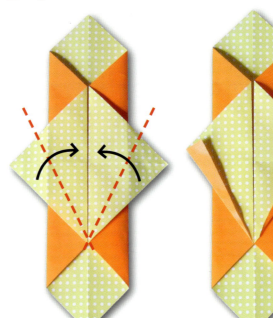

STEP 5:
Next, fold up the bottom of the model toward the right-hand side so that the left-hand edge meets the right-hand side point. Crease hard and unfold. Then repeat on the other side.

The left-hand edge should meet the right-hand side point.

The right-hand edge should meet the left-hand side point.

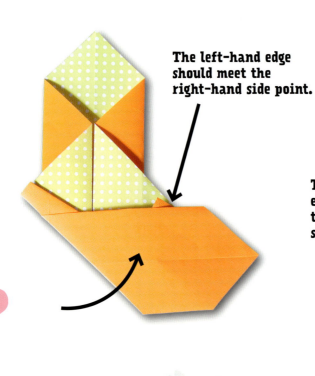

STEP 6:

Fold up the bottom point of the model along the red dotted line. As you make this fold, open out the two flaps along the black dotted lines. The creases you made in step 5 will make this possible.

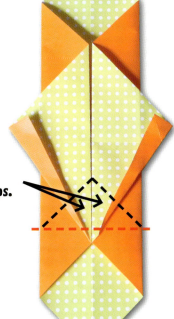

Flatten the bottom of the model. It should now look like this.

STEP 7:

Fold the bottom point back down, and crease.

bottom point

STEP 8:

To make the teddy bear's arms, fold in the two side points of the model, and crease.

STEP 9:

Fold the top of the model down to make the teddy bear's head, and crease. Tuck the point under to make the bear's chin.

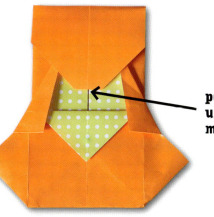

point tucked under to make chin

29

STEP 10:

Turn the model over. Fold up the bottom of the model, and crease hard.

To make the bear's ears, fold each top corner down, and crease hard. Then fold the corner back up again to make a small pleat.

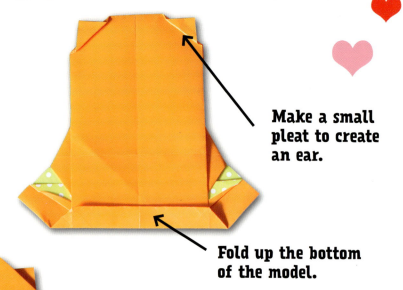

Make a small pleat to create an ear.

Fold up the bottom of the model.

STEP 11:

Turn the model back over, draw on a face, and the teddy bear is complete!

STEP 12:

To make the heart, take a piece of paper that's a quarter of the size of the piece used to make the teddy bear. Place the paper colored side down. Fold in half from one side to the other, crease, and unfold. Then fold in half from top to bottom, crease and unfold—exactly as you did to start the teddy bear.

Next, fold down the top point to meet the center, and crease.

Then fold up the bottom point to meet the top of the model, and crease.

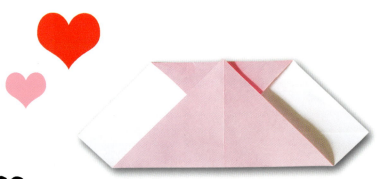

STEP 13:
Fold in each side of the model along the dotted lines so they meet at the center crease, and crease well.

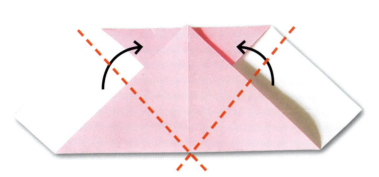

STEP 14:
Turn the model over. Fold in the two side points, and crease. Fold down the two top points, and crease. Then turn the heart over and write your message on it.

Slide the heart into the teddy bear's arms. You can use a little glue to hold it in place. Happy Valentine's Day!

Glossary

fortune
A person's future destiny. Also, the word for a large amount of money or valuable possessions.

origami
The art of folding paper into decorative shapes or objects.

romantic
Having to do with being in love.

symbol
Something that stands for or represents another thing, such as an important event or person. For example, a heart shape is a symbol of love.

unique
One of a kind.

Index

A
Aphrodite, 10

E
envelope model, 22–23, 24–25

F
fortune-teller origami model, 18–19, 20–21
fortune-telling, 4, 18

H
hearts, 4, 7, 8, 14, 26

J
Japan, 4

L
love letters, 4, 22

O
origami (general), 4, 6–7

R
rose origami model, 10–11, 12–13
roses, 7, 10

S
striped love heart model, 8–9

T
teddy bears, 4, 26
teddy bear with heart origami model, 26–27, 28–29, 30–31

V
Venus, 10

W
winged heart origami model, 14–15, 16–17

Websites

www.easypeasyandfun.com/valentines-day-crafts-for-kids/
www.inthekidskitchen.com/valentines-day-treats-kids/
www.origami-instructions.com/origami-hearts.html

Publisher's note to educators and parents: Our editors have carefully reviewed these websites to ensure that they are suitable for students. Many websites change frequently, however, and we cannot guarantee that a site's future contents will continue to meet our high standards of quality and educational value. Be advised that students should be closely supervised whenever they access the internet.